Working Stiffs

Working Stiffs

Stories
by George Dila

One Wet Shoe Publishing 2014

Published by   One Wet Shoe Publishing
                 1709 W Lyons Street
                 Mount Pleasant, MI 48858
                 www.onewetshoe.com

ISBN 978-0-989607-12-4

ACKNOWLEDGMENTS
The author acknowledges the following journals where these stories
first appeared:

Driftwood Journal: "90 Million"
North American Review: "Shaft Men"
Per Contra Journal: "Eyes to Wonder, Tongues to Praise"

Cover designed by Marie Marfia/Dancing Mac Graphics. Book
designed and typeset by Amee Schmidt with titles in Helvetica Neue
and text in Minion Pro. Author photo courtesy of Deb Dila.

Contents

For Chaz and Kristie

Eyes to Wonder, Tongues to Praise

The sounds of Harry being murdered in the office at the end of the hall are the only sounds. The grunts, the thumps. The muffled expletives. No mercy. Harry being murdered, surrounded by a violent hush, breaths held, paper shuffling stopped, conversations ended in mid-word, typewriters stilled. I, like the others who hear the murder being committed, am helpless to save poor Harry, so I withdraw to the black space behind my eyes, my own private terror hole, a cold hand taking hold of my heart. Even the telephones seem to understand. *Don't ring 'til old Harry's dead. Show some respect.* James Francis Bigelow, Director of Marketing, a.k.a. The Singing Assassin, a.k.a. The Prince of Fucking Darkness, murdering poor Harry for some fuck-up or other, most likely an honest mistake, maybe Harry's or somebody else's, it doesn't matter, Harry's intestines torn out, his testicles ripped off, his head battered to jelly, no problem, Harry will bounce back, be here tomorrow, resurrected with his famous grin on, and that's how it really is here at the office, and nobody who ever described it got it right.

* * *

This is one of our favorite pranks. You stick your head into somebody's office, let's say Pringle's, and you say, "Hey, Pringle, Bigelow wants to see you," and you watch Pringle's face go white, Pringle's shoulders slump, and then you say, "Just kidding, Pringle."

"Bastard," he says, turning back to his computer screen.

Harmless fun among the lads, kid's stuff, but look out, you may be next.

* * *

Introductions all around. You met Bigelow the murderer and Harry the grinner and Pringle the trembler. Then there's Weiss, Hogwood, Tyrell, Struhberg and Smith. I'm Baker. Struhberg's a *she*, the only one except for assorted and sundry secretaries and assistants. Tyrell's black, irrelevant, but true.

We're the *Direct Marketing/Domestic Markets* management team. We each supervise a half-dozen or so underlings.

There was one more. Margolis. A crazyman. Self-destructive. We were friends.

Margolis and I are coming back from lunch one day, walking through the lobby of the building, and there, heading out the door, is the president of the company, the guy whose name is on the checks, let's call him Mr. Big. I've met Mr. Big twice before, at company Christmas parties. He doesn't know Margolis or me from Adam. He rarely ventures off the 15th floor. I've never been past the 14th—Human Resources.

So Margolis walks up to him and says, "Hello, sir. I'm Margolis."

Mr. Big puts on a smile, sticks out his hand for a shake and says, "Real nice to see you again, Margolis."

"We've never met, sir," Margolis says, pumping the presidential hand.

"Really," Mr. Big says, pumping back.

"You know, sir, you and I have something in common," Margolis says, his eyes popping with excitement.

This stops Mr. Big for a fraction of a second, his smile slips the slightest bit, then comes back on full.

"Really?" he asks with a hearty, just-one-of-the-boys laugh. "How's that Margolis?"

"Neither of us is going any further in this company," Margolis says. "We've both gone about as far as we can go."

That afternoon Margolis is called to the 14th floor. Human Resources. We never see him again.

* * *

I have this dream.

A boy comes to the door. I know him but I *don't* know him. He is strange and familiar at the same time.

He hands me a note and runs off. Now I am in the empty street, looking for the address written on the note. It is a shack. I knock. A man opens the door. It is the boy, grown up. His face is blank. He has no eyes, no nose, no mouth. He says, "Hello, Baker."

The man is me.

* * *

What we market here is computers, but it could be anything. Cars. Candles. Curious George dolls. Couches. Carpet. Canned goods. Condominiums. Condoms. It wouldn't matter.

* * *

Staff meeting. Tuesday. 8 a.m. We file into the conference room. Bigelow waits at the head of the table, singing "The Impossible Dream," dramatically imitating Richard Kiley, manicured hands clasped at his chest. He has washed them clean of blood stains. His silver Breitling softly embraces his wrist above a starched, white French cuff held in place by a diamond-studded cuff link in the shape of dice.

Behind Bigelow sits Mary Beth, his secretary. She'll take notes, make a report of the meeting. Harry is at the other end of the table, good as new. Grin in place. There are two empty chairs. Smith is on vacation. Margolis has been disappeared.

Bigelow abruptly stops singing.

"Where's Smith?" he asks, the corners of his mouth turned up in an approximation of a smile. He knows where Smith is, but he asks anyway.

"Vacation," someone finally says, although no lips have moved.

"Vacation," Bigelow says, shaking his head, letting us know that he considers vacations undeserved remnants of a decaying, decadent system.

"He'll be back Monday," someone volunteers.

"Maybe," says Bigelow, narrowing his eyes. He glances over his shoulder at Mary Beth. "So, let's have reports."

There is a pause. Harry-the-resurrected fills it.

"Mr. B, we have a problem with independent dealer incentives," he says. *Hey, I'm still alive and kicking*, is the real message he's sending.

Bigelow's eyes move to Tyrell. Dealer Incentives is Tyrell's baby. Tyrell gives Harry a quick, nasty look.

"It's . . . " Tyrell clears his throat. "It's not really a problem, as such," he says, his normal basso escalating to tenor.

"As such?" Bigelow asks.

"The D-Gs (Dealer-Groups to the uninitiated) don't care for the trips. They tell me they're tired of the trips."

"Fuck the D-Gs," Bigelow says. He takes a slim leather case from his breast pocket, slides out of it a gold toothpick and begins cleaning his teeth with the damned thing. I look away.

Harry jumps in again.

"That's what I told Tyrell, Mr. B," he says. "Fuck the D-Gs!"

Bigelow asks for a pencil. Three pencils immediately skitter toward him across the smooth table-top. He ignores them all.

"By the way, where's Margolis?" he asks with mock innocence, arching his eyebrows.

Nobody answers. Bigelow is the only person in the room who actually knows where Margolis is, where the body is buried. He thinks of his question as a little joke. A bit of levity to lighten up the meeting.

And so it goes.

Tyrell takes a few more hits on the Dealer-Groups thing. Struhberg keeps her mouth shut when Bigelow refers to the women in the department as "the girls." Harry, grinning, brings up a problem with sales commissions, causing Hogwood to take a few hits. Bigelow asks again where Smith is. "Vacation," he says, shaking his head, answering his own question. Pringle gives a sleep-inducing report on a new wireless telephone system for the office.

Bigelow says, "Forget new phones."

Pringle says, "But it was your idea, Mr. B." (We all call Bigelow *Mr. B*.) Six month's work for Pringle, down the crapper.

Weiss and I come out of the meeting untouched. Harry is the big winner. He grins. Bigelow's teeth are clean. He breaks into "I've Grown Accustomed to Her Face," speak-singing *a la* Rex Harrison.

* * *

That afternoon Bigelow shouts down the hall, "Baker!"

I call back, "Yo!"

When summoned to Bigelow's office, each of us moves at our own carefully calculated speed. Pringle is the fastest. He has hung up the phone on his wife, stomped on feet, and knocked over waste baskets in his rush to get out of his office and down the hall. We are all embarrassed for Pringle. I move at a more measured pace, not too fast, not too slow.

As I walk into his office, he is Zero Mostel singing "If I Were a Rich Man." He stops singing.

"Shut the door," he says. "Sit." As if I am a dog.

I shut the door. I sit. I face him across an uncluttered expanse of polished rosewood.

"What's up?" I ask.

"Tyrell. What'd'ya think of him?"

I sense danger.

"He's a good guy," I say. Bigelow makes a snorting noise. I continue. "He's smart. Manages his people well. Why?"

"He's a fuck-up."

"I don't agree. Harry sand-bagged him at the staff meeting."

Bigelow looks at me like you'd look at an idiot son.

"You think I don't know Harry's tricks. You think I don't see the shit he pulls, making people look bad. Give me more credit, Baker, for Christ sake." He polishes his glasses with the end of his tie. "So what'd'ya think of Tyrell, really?"

"A fuck-up," I admit.

"Like I said," says Bigelow.

"But Dealer-Groups is tough. It's hard to keep them happy."

"Hell yes, it's hard. If it was easy one of the girls would do it."

I don't respond to that. We're both quiet for a while. I warn myself to stay alert.

Bigelow says, "Tyrell is gone. Consider him history. I'm giving you Dealer-Groups. You can pick your own team. You up to it?"

"Sure, I'm up to it." Without hesitation.

"We'll see. You handle this, it's a big step for you, Baker."

"I understand."

"So, you want the job or not?" asks the Prince of Fucking Darkness. "I wanna hear you say it."

I try to imagine Bigelow as a kid. A sweet, innocent kid. Fresh-faced. Wide-eyed. Loving. He was one once. Had to be. Weren't we all?

"Of course I want the job," I say.

On the credenza behind Bigelow is a hinged, two-panel silver picture frame. In one panel is a formal portrait of a placid, middle-aged woman with carefully arranged blond hair. In the facing panel, two kids careen recklessly down a swimming pool slide, gleeful smiles for their daddy on their glistening faces. Not the devil. A family man.

I have similar pictures on my desk. A woman. A boy with a dog.

"Good. Now, get outta here. And be nice to Tyrell." Bigelow's wink strikes me as obscene. "He won't be here tomorrow."

I begin to push out of the chair, then hesitate, open my mouth to speak, then close it, indecision causing my brain to short-circuit. Bigelow has not noticed. He's already forgotten me, busily searching for something in a drawer, singing to himself, "If Ever I Would Leave You," in the manner of Robert Goulet.

What is it that I want to say? Thanks? Thanks for the opportunity, the bigger job, probably bigger pay? Or, do I want to tell him that I am different from the others—smarter than Margolis, stronger than Tyrell, more resilient than Harry, braver than Pringle. Or, am I afraid to leave his office, face my comrades, afraid something will show on my face, some sign of my betrayal.

Back in my office.

Tyrell comes in, closes the door, sits down in one of my guest chairs. He clears his throat, getting his basso ready. His forehead shines like polished mahogany. A tic works at the corner of his eye.

"You were just in with Bigelow," he says.

I feel his fear across the desk.

"Yeah?"

He waits for me to continue. I don't. Instead, I shove a pencil into my electric sharpener. When the grinding stops, he says, "Damn Harry! Making me look bad in the meeting! Did Bigelow mention that?"

"He told me he knows Harry's tricks."

"What'd he say about me?"

"Nothing."

"Come on, Baker. What'd he say about me? He tells you shit. You're his favorite little boy."

This comment irritates me, but I don't let Tyrell see it.

"Trust me, Tyrell. He didn't say anything. Your name didn't come up." I am lying fluidly now, seamlessly. I lean back in my chair. "I'm sure he knows you're doing the best you can with the D-Gs." My eyes fall on the pictures on my desk. My wife and son smile back.

"I'm doing better than anybody ever did with the fucking D-Gs. But it's a thankless task." His voice has taken on an unpleasant whine. "I should never have agreed to take 'em. When he asked me a year ago, I should have said no."

An hour later I see Tyrell waiting for the elevator. He is facing the etched bronze doors, standing perfectly, utterly, rigidly still, hands clasped at his back as if handcuffed. I sense that, with enormous effort, he is holding himself under control, afraid that if he moves even a finger he will shatter into a million pieces.

The bronze doors open. Tyrell moves into the elevator and the doors close. The glowing arrow indicates UP. I suspect that I have seen him for the last time.

The next day I inherit his office and the D-Gs.

* * *

Coffee room. Monday. 10 a.m. Smith is back from vacation.

"Where's Tyrell?" he asks. "I haven't seen him this morning."

"Among the missing," Struhberg answers. "Since last Tuesday afternoon."

Smith blinks nervously, sensing that something awful happened while he was gone, but not knowing *what* or if it affects him, or if he's in trouble. Harry has his biggest grin on.

"Baker's in charge of D-Gs now," Harry says. "About time we had somebody worth a shit in that slot."

His compliment, if that's what it is, does not warm me. Smith blinks harder. Any salubrious effect of his vacation has abruptly vanished.

* * *

Some weeks later. Friday. 9 a.m.

From my desk I can see down the hall to the elevators. I watch as the bronze doors slide open, revealing, what? My brain needs a few seconds to make sense of it. Stepping out of the elevator, side-by-side, are Tyrell and Margolis. Both wear long, black topcoats and blank expressions. No one notices but me. The doors close behind them and the elevator moves off with a soft *bong*.

Am I dreaming?

Margolis and Tyrell glance at each other, then reach inside their coats and slowly, deliberately withdraw identical handguns. I know nothing about guns but these look like very serious weapons to me, large, smooth, efficient killing machines of modern design, the ultimate high-tech examples of the gun-maker's craft.

I am mesmerized by the sight, too stunned to speak or call out. A small sound, part gurgle, part grunt, escapes my throat. My hand, only a few inches from the telephone, is lead. Too heavy to move.

The two men pause for a moment, standing in an identical, vaguely military position, like something they've learned, their guns held flat against their chests, muzzles angled toward the ceiling. Then, almost in unison, they lower their weapons and, with a quick, practiced movement, work some kind of cocking mechanism. WRACK! is the sound it makes. I cannot move or speak, but now I notice that my mind is screaming, NO! Still, no one has seen them but me.

Now, as if they have rehearsed, they turn back-to-back and begin moving together down the hall, Margolis facing the offices on my side and Tyrell facing the offices on the other side, guns held straight out, in firing position. Struhberg and Pringle, in the offices closest to the elevators, will die first. I hear a high squeak of surprise, probably Struhberg, and then the killing begins.

The guns make a terrible sound, a dull thudding that echoes along the hallway. There are shouts. There is running. There is wood cracking and glass shattering. And there is the awful smell, a combination of burning and blood and fear. Finally, Margolis stands at my open door.

"Baker!" he says, a smile breaking across his face. "Baker, I thought you'd be long gone from this dump."

My brain feels like it's wrapped in cotton wool. I try to focus on the pictures on my desk. I think I say his name. "Margolis."

"Baker, you gotta get the hell outta this joint. It ain't worth the hassle, man."

Tyrell, busy killing Smith across the way, doesn't notice as Margolis lifts his weapon and fires four rounds into the wall above my head. He winks as he slaps a new clip into his gun, then moves to the next office. Harry dies, begging for his life, no grin on.

They reach the office at the end of the hall, the scene of so many murders. Bigelow will be the last to die. I hear him bellowing, "Oh What a Beautiful Morning," bravely, I think, imitating Gordon McRae, and then the fusillade, both men emptying their guns into our despised leader.

It is quiet. I have not moved from behind my desk. I hear Margolis and Tyrell coming back down the hall, Tyrell saying, "I'm gonna check out Baker, make sure he's dead. That motherfucker got my job."

And Margolis tells him, "I made sure, Bro. He's deader than hell. Trust me."

And Tyrell, coming closer, says, "I ain't taking any chances. He stabbed me in the back, man. Got my office and my job."

Still I cannot move, and now he is at my door.

"Hey, Baker!"

He's found me, alive.

"Hey, Baker, what's your problem? You look like you seen a ghost, pal. You okay?"

It is Harry, with his grin on. I focus on his face.

"I guess I was daydreaming," I say. "About Tyrell and Margolis. You ever wonder what happened to 'em, Harry?"

"Don't know, don't give a shit! But I *do* know the Prince wants to see you."

"Yeah, sure," I say, assuming that Harry's playing our game. "Tell Caruso I'm busy. I'll catch his act later."

"Baker, look at me. I'm not kidding. This is not a kidding face. The boss wants to see you. I wouldn't keep him waiting if I were you."

When I walk into Bigelow's office a minute later he is thumbing through a stack of computer print-outs, singing "Some Enchanted Evening" like Ezio Pinza. . . "strange-ooorr". . . rolling his Rs with gusto.

"The numbers look good, Baker," he says, letting the stack of print-outs drop to the desk. "Looks like we're making some headway with the D-Gs."

"They like the new product line. They're juiced up about the new incentives, too."

"You've caught their eye on the 15th floor, Baker. The big boys. They like what you're doing. Don't fuck up."

"I think I have things under control."

"Having a little success is a double-edged sword, chum. It gets you noticed. But then we expect more. You're in the spotlight. If you screw up, everybody knows."

"Is this a pep talk?"

He ignores my sarcasm. "Ever been on the 15th floor Baker?"

"No, sir."

"The 15th floor gives new meaning to the word *extravagant*, Baker. Posh. The old man," he says, referring to Mr. Big, "likes his creature comforts."

"Uh-huh."

"Fresh flowers on every desk. Carpeting this thick." He shows me with his fingers. "Art on the walls. Not cheap prints. Originals. Oils."

"Sounds great."

"They tried to get me to move up there a couple of years ago. I said *no*. They told me they wanted all the execs on the same floor. I told them I wanted to stay here with my people."

"Well, it's nice to have you so close," I say with a tiny smile.

He returns the smile, this casual intimacy our little secret. "Yeah, sure." He chuckles. "I use an old fashioned management technique, Baker. Fear. It works for me. People seem to respond to it. But you're not afraid of me, are you, Baker.?

"No, sir, I'm not."

"As I thought." He glances at his Breitling. "So, any questions?"

I pause, consider hard before saying, "Just one. What ever happened to Margolis?"

"Hm, Margolis," Bigelow says thoughtfully, nodding, "Friend of yours, right?"

"We were friends."

"He never got in touch with you, huh?"

"Never heard from him."

"That's usually how it is. We seldom hear from 'em again."

"So he just got fired?"

"Margolis had potential. Smart kid. But crazy. Reckless."

"Harmless," I add.

Bigelow nods. "Yeah, probably. If you want, I can find out where he is. Let you know."

"Sure." I don't ask about Tyrell.

He glances at his desk calendar. He is finished with me.

"Tell Pringle I want to see him."

I walk down the hall feeling, what? An odd mixture of emotions. Giddiness, with a touch of foreboding and a dash of spite. My steps feel light, as if I am walking on the moon. I stick my head into Pringle's office.

"Pringle, the boss wants to see you," I say. "I'm not kidding this time."

I don't wait to see his reaction. The games are over.

* * *

I have this dream. I am alone on a stage, facing a crowd of thousands. Spotlights sweep the stage in great, bright arcs, as if searching for an escaped prisoner. Each beam stops when it finds me, and finally I am pinned in a blinding, burning circle of light.

I open my mouth and begin to sing.

Shaft Men

When we reached the Jordan River it was the middle of the night, the guys were beat, and grumbling about the forced march, but as Shem says to me, orders is orders.

Joshua, the fanatic that he is, has to control every last detail, the rest of us are jackasses, everybody from his lieutenants on down to the lowest shaft men like me and Shem and Dov and Rube. A bunch of incompetents who couldn't lace their own sandals in the dark. So he's going around with that voice of his, like a lion's roar, stomping, dust flying, civilians in that valley over there, troops here, pointing with his sword, command post by the river, sleeping tents on that hill, meeting tents by those trees, spittle flying as he roars, chariots over there, where Cookie's supposed to set up the chow tent, and so forth. And most of us just want to drop where we are and sleep, but latrines must be dug first, Joshua's orders.

Finally he's satisfied that the camp's the way he wants it. Everything's always the way he wants it, but of course he says it's the way Yahweh wants it, and Dov says, how can you argue with that?

The next morning Shem says they're raising a special tent in the middle of camp, and a priest passes me. I am sitting, polishing my shaft, my name burned into it near the handle, sharpening the point with my stone, and the priest winks, like he knows something I don't, and another priest on his way to the special tent smirks, and Shem says, I don't like this at all. Not one bit.

All the men are lined up, twenty lines going into the tent, we're well back, but I hear screaming and wailing from the tent, and then the word comes, the priests are cutting the skin off the end of our most private part, Rube says, like Moses did to all the men, back, what? oh, forty or fifty years. Shem says to me, we are going to be lesser shaft men when we come out of the tent; that is Shem's humor. I can't believe how Dov squalls like a baby when it's his turn. I just grit my teeth and only grunt once, but tears do come to my eyes, I can't help that. It takes four weeks to heal. There is nothing for us to do but polish our shafts and practice thrusts and blocks, and every time I go to the latrine to do my water, I cannot believe what I hold in my hand.

* * *

Word comes that we will take Jericho, across the Jordan. Training begins. Shem, Dov, Rube and I make up one rank of shaft men, going into battle elbow to elbow, shafts in ready position. We have never been in battle before.

We practice shafting drills. Death to Canaanites! Die Canaanite! Canaanite Dog! These are some of the curses we are encouraged to yell as we charge and drive our shafts into the straw dummy Canaanites. For Yahweh! For the promised land! Remember Egypt!

At the campfire the night before we are to move across the river, Rube tells me he is afraid. Shem tells me he is ready to kill Canaanites. Dov tells me he may try some of that Canaanite pussy. Be careful of disease, I tell him.

It has been a dry summer, the river low. We move across in ranks of four, led by the priests carrying the ark, then priests with horns, then archers, then swordsmen, then shaft men, then utility men. Fifty thousand strong.

On the horizon Jericho is a small brown blur, changing shape in the heat waves that rise off the blistered plain. We march towards it. We will do Yahweh's great work beneath a good blue sky. We sing. Yahweh is great. Yahweh is powerful. The Canaanites must cower in their sandals watching our great army advance upon them. They fear us. They fear Yahweh. And when they hear us singing, their terror will grow. We are confident of victory.

As we march, Jericho grows, and when we reach it, it is like a mountain in our path.

Holy shit, Rube says, staring up at the wall, his eyes big as water pots.

Our squad leader, Jeb, gives our rank a dirty look. Shut your hole, Dov tells Rube.

We march all the way around the city, singing, and the sound of each step, fifty thousand sandals hitting the ground at once, brings awe even to me. When we complete the march the horns blare, it is a mighty sound. We are a mighty army, and I hope the Canaanites are as convinced as I am.

We set up camp an arrow's flight from the wall. Shem guesses that Joshua and his lieutenants are sizing things up, figuring out how, for the love of Abraham, we are going to get into the city to sack it. For Yahweh.

The next morning we form up and march around Jericho again. Our feet thud, we sing, the horns blare. We return to camp. Do not question authority, Jeb tells us. There is a plan.

The next day we march around the city again, and the next day, and the next, and the next. The spring is gone from our step, the gusto from our voices. Shem asks, How many officers does it take to lead an ass? I cannot repeat his answer.

On the sixth night the buzz around the campfire is that Joshua is in a foul mood.

It is still dark when we are rousted from our warm beds the next morning. We form up in the quavering light of a thousand torches. Something will happen today, Dov whispers. Yes, I agree. It will happen today.

We begin the march with our shafts held straighter, our heads higher. As we march, the sky lightens over the distant hills, then the sun comes quickly and for a few moments the wall of Jericho is blood red. When we complete one circle of the city we do not go back to camp but continue marching. By the time the sun is overhead we have marched around the city three times and the men are taking long pulls at their water skins. Bugger a camel, Shem mutters. That's a tight plan, Rube gives back grimly. By the fifth circling of the city men are stumbling, collapsing in the dust. We pass nearly a hundred who have been dragged to the side and left, like old, useless dogs. We continue marching. By the seventh circling of the city the butt end of my shaft drags the ground. My goat skin bottle, nearly empty, thumps against my belly. Madness, Shem mutters. Madness.

Then word comes down the line. Joshua wants louder singing. Great idea, says Shem, rolling his eyes. That'll do the trick, says Dov. Shut your hole, says our squad leader, Jeb. We sing louder, angry, and now, from the front of the march, the horns begin a continuous blasting, furious, relentless blasting. And now, new word comes down the line. Begin shouting. Shout without ceasing. Shout louder than you have ever shouted before. We are creating a terrible din, we are working ourselves into a fury, and suddenly the ranks begin to move faster, and then faster still, and soon we are circling the wall at a dead run, shouting, feet thudding, horns blaring, and as we round the curve of the wall we see that the city's main gate is open and our army is pouring through. Half the army must be inside by the time we reach the gate and we thunder through, trying to stay in our rank of four, and we are shouting Death, Death to Canaanites, Canaanite Dogs!

Our army has scattered into every sector of the city. There are fires everywhere, shouts of victory and screams of death, and the smell of blood and fear. Every street, every building, every house must be entered, destroyed, every person killed, every possession burned, Yahweh has commanded it. Our squad pounds down a narrow street following our leader; there are small houses close on both sides, but no Canaanites, not a soul, and our leader yells, Inside! Inside! and Dov and I rush through an open door, looking for the enemy. There is no one in the first room. Dov and I stop, breathing hard. We listen. Then he makes a gesture with his head, telling me to go through one door, he will go through the other. I nod agreement. I lift my shaft to ready position. As I advance towards the door I slowly turn the weapon in my hands until I can see my name, Samuel, etched by fire. I enter the small room, look, then turn and come back out, my shaft clean. Dov is coming out of his room. No one, he says. No one, I say. Shit! says Dov.

We return to the smoky street. My eyes smart, my throat is tight, my mouth gritty. I can still see, as if the image is real, the four people huddled in the corner of the room I had entered, their faces turned towards me in terror, their eyes wide. The old man, toothless, his skin as brown and withered as an olive leaf on the winter ground. The mother, her lips moving quickly in silent speech, holding a shaking boy against her, her hand clamped across his mouth. The girl, soft as ripe fruit, reaching forward, offering in her sweet palm, a ring of hammered gold. I will never forget them, the Canaanite dogs.

* * *

Reports that the wall of Jericho fell down are untrue, impossible, as you'd know if you ever saw that wall. The truth is that the gates had been opened from the inside by Joshua's spies.

We left Jericho and kept fighting, laying waste the cities, taking what was ours, what was promised, and here are the Kings we defeated, and their people, who were either Hittites or Amorites or Canaanites or Perizzites or Hivites or Jebusites.

The King of Jericho
The King of Ai, near Bethel
The King of Jerusalem
The King of Hebron
The King of Jarmuth
The King of Lachish
The King of Eglon
The King of Gezer
The King of Debir
The King of Geder
The King of Hormah
The King of Arad
The King of Libnah
The King of Adullam
The King of Makkedah
The King of Bethel
The King of Tappu-ah
The King of Hepher
The King of Aphek
The King of Lasharon

The King of Madon
The King of Hazor
The King of Shimron-miron
The King of Achshaph
The King of Tannach
The King of Megiddo
The King of Kedesh
The King of Jokne-am
The King of Dor
The King of Goriim in Gilgal
The King of Tirzah

I became a squad leader, and then a troop leader. A leader of shaft men. The notches on my shaft, for all those I've killed, are too numerous to count.

90 Million

Martin Harpoonian had no sooner finished signing his name to the dozen or so documents placed ceremoniously before him on the conference table, and received in exchange ninety million dollars for the purchase of his company, Harpco Molds and Plastics, than he closed his eyes, lowered his head, leaned close to his lawyer, Meyer Kottman, and whispered, "Tell them I changed my mind. Tell them to keep their fucking money."

I, Howard Barnacle, Assistant to the President of Harpco, witnessed this moment—possibly I alone. Others gathered around the long table of the Bank of Commerce executive board room were too busy to notice—otherwise occupied talking into iPhones, rummaging in thousand-dollar Dunhill briefcases, guzzling Evian, thoughtfully provided by the bank's hospitality director. And this is how the extraordinary moment had occurred. Harpoonian had checked the time on his twenty thousand dollar gold Ebel, then signed away his company with his own fifty-nine cent Bic. Followed by the pause, eyes closed, and the blunt, whispered instruction.

"It was the fastest case of seller's remorse I've ever seen," Kottman told me weeks later.

Harpoonian, pushing hard at seventy, was still a tidy hundred and forty pounds, a feisty welterweight with a good head of silver hair, and a pencil-thin mustache, carefully trimmed, beneath his grand Armenian nose.

Actually, he had received a check for only ten million, with notes, stocks, and other compensation making up the balance of the ninety million, for tax purposes, he said, as his "Jew lawyers and Jew accountants" had advised him.

"Too late to return it, Marty," Meyer Kottman whispered back. "You're a very rich man, whether you like it or not."

"I been rich for years."

"Not like this, Marty." The lawyer squeezed his client's arm through the sleeve of his silk sport coat. "Ninety million."

Harpoonian slammed his own briefcase shut, a fat, beat-up twenty-dollar job he'd used for years. One Christmas soon after I'd come to work at Harpco, Harpoonian's wife had given him a slim new calfskin case, the color mellow as polished rosewood. I'd done my new boss the favor of returning it to the store and bringing the cash back to him, more money than I was paying for a month's rent at the time.

"Mr. Harpoonian." It was one of the men from the holding company, 21st Century America, that had just paid him ninety million for Harpco Molds and Plastics, a tall, MBA-type in gray flannel and wingtips, named Wolfe. He would be running the place soon. "Marty," he said, "the agreement calls for immediate possession. We don't want to rush you, but we need to get into your office, start the transition."

Harpoonian called to me abruptly, "Barnacle!" and gestured with his head toward the door.

"By Monday, Marty?" Wolfe asked. "That gives you two days plus the weekend. Any problem with that?"

"I'll let you know," Harpoonian said. He put his lips close to his lawyer's ear. "Have a nice day, you hymie bastard," I heard him whisper.

"Ninety million, you schmuck," Meyer Kottman whispered back. "Not bad for a guy who can barely read."

Harpoonian headed for the door, chin out, his briefcase swinging. I followed a step behind, carrying mine.

* * *

The Harpco headquarters was a lump, a potato of a building, two stories of brown brick attached to the front of our suburban

Detroit plant. The executive wing was a single hallway with offices on both sides. Each office door had a window onto the hallway, so people couldn't hide out or snooze. My office was next to Harpoonian's, separated only by the thickness of a couple of fake wood grain panels. That evening, I waited until the rest of the staff had left the building, then joined him in his office. The only place for guests was a flimsy Danish modern sofa of teak wood and thin pads that had probably been salvaged from the Harpoonian's family room after a redecorating. Likewise, a mammoth old console TV with a set of rabbit ears that pulled in fuzzy black and white pictures from two local stations.

"Well Marty," I said. "You did alright for yourself."

He was slouched in his big leather swivel chair, sullen as a schoolboy. The chair was the one office luxury he allowed himself. "For my back," he'd told me.

"Yeah, and now what?" he asked, and then after a pause, "How long you been with me, Barnacle?"

"Fifteen years," I answered. "Around there."

I'd started as an assistant office manager. Now I had an elevated title and a fat salary, but I was still doing whatever Harpoonian asked me to do—answering complaints from customers, recruiting office help, keeping an eye on expense reports, planning executive meetings and company picnics. I was a sounding board, a confidant, a lightning rod. Running errands. Keeping my eyes and ears open. Doing favors.

"Fifteen years. It seems like you just started."

"So what are your plans, Marty?" I asked. "Going to take some time off?"

"You heard that asshole at the closing? That tall guy with those fruity glasses." Harpoonian made finger circles around his eyes.

"Wolfe," I said.

"Yeah, that guy. He wants immediate possession. Out by Monday." He gestured around the room. "What am I gonna do with all this junk in three days?"

His office was like his briefcase; unpretentious, disorganized. The desk was massive, gray metal, maybe from World War II. Every square inch was covered. Reports, trade magazines, contracts, resumes, letters, scribbled notes, paper stacked a foot high in spots, piles leaning into each other, some collapsed into chaotic heaps. Hanging from nails hammered into the wall behind the desk were a half-dozen clipboards holding thick computer printouts generated by the IT Department, but he hated computers and refused to have one in his office. In a corner were two battered file cabinets, their olive drab paint worn through to bare metal in spots, crammed with useless stuff going back decades, invoices and receipts and leases and who knows what? And there was more stuff—on top of the file cabinets and the TV set, on the floor, along the edges of the room, stacked in corners, pieces of molded plastic, some identifiable, like lopsided bottles and grotesquely distorted, brightly colored toys, but most unidentifiable, misshapen fragments, scraps, rejected jobs, the flotsam and jetsam of decades in the molded plastics trade. Some of the stuff had been in the room when I interviewed for my job, fifteen years before.

"You don't need any of this, do you?" I said.

"Need? Need?" He closed his eyes and was quiet for so long I thought he'd dozed off. Harpoonian's work schedule was legendary. He went to bed very late every night, got up early every morning, terrified of being caught asleep, dreaming, while his hated competition or his untrustworthy suppliers might be up, awake, getting the better of him. He made up for this with little thirty-second cat naps during the day. I waited. I'd waited before. Finally, he opened his eyes. "Did I ever tell you about my mother?"

I'd listened to Martin Harpoonian talk about his beloved mother many times in the past fifteen years. He talked frequently about *his* family, *his* marriage, *his* history, *his* life as if it were more interesting or consequential than others. I had never told him about *my* mother. It had never occurred to me to do so. It had never occurred to me to tell him about *my* family, about my ex-wife Elizabeth, about my marriage, my son. And he never asked.

"My mother was the smartest woman I ever knew," Harpoonian said. "And the hardest working."

I'd met her just once. When I first came to work at Harpco, he had invited me to his house for dinner. Mother Harpoonian, who was living with Marty and his family, seemed hale and hearty, white-haired but tall and straight, her hawk nose intimidating, her black eyes flashing. But in truth, she was in the middle stages of Alzheimer's, and she spent the whole dinner giggling and tossing pieces of bread across the table at me.

"Mother!" Harpoonian would say, "Cut it out!" Harshly, but lovingly.

I pretended not to notice.

Also at the dinner table had been Harpoonian's wife, Ethel, fresh from a visit to her hair colorist, and their teenaged son Jack, a fat, pampered lout who grunted and ate with his mouth open. That was fifteen years ago. Now, mother Harpoonian was in the ground, Jack was a Vice President of Harpco, with kids of his own, and Ethel spent most of her time in New York, living in the apartment they'd bought near Lincoln Center, shopping on 5th Avenue.

Harpoonian moved to the edge of his chair, leaned closer to me across the desk, and spoke in a quiet voice.

"When my father died, my mother had to support us. I was just a kid. She'd go downtown someplace and buy this household stuff wholesale. Potato peelers, vegetable brushes, dish rags, kitchen junk. Then she'd go door-to-door, walk all day, selling this stuff. That's how she supported us. We—" Harpoonian's voice caught in his throat. "We never went hungry."

It always took him a minute or two to recover from these reminiscences. I waited, giving him time.

"I wish I could have known mother Harpoonian better," I said finally.

He looked at me as if questioning my sincerity, then seemed to push the errant thought aside.

"Right," he said. "So, what do I do with all this stuff?"

"You don't need it, Marty. Just throw it out."

"Just pitch it? Thirty-five years worth?"

"So save a few personal things and toss the rest. What's in these file cabinets, anyway? Nothing the new guys need. Like all of us here. Excess baggage."

"I told those assholes they were crazy if they let you go," he said.

"I know. I appreciate it."

"But there's no telling what the dumb bastards will do. They know nothing about plastic. Just about counting beans. The bottom line."

"The bottom line," I said.

"And they don't care about people. Devious."

"That's what they learn in business school, I guess."

"You should be okay for six months, at least. It'll take 'em that long to find the bathroom."

"At least."

"I've always taken care of you, haven't I?"

"You've never gone back on a promise, Marty."

"If they let you go I'll help you find something."

"I'll be okay."

We were both quiet for a while. I considered going, leaving him alone with his own thoughts about this place that was his, that was the essence of him, this place he'd practically lived in for thirty-five years. I stared down at my shoes.

Suddenly, I was jerked out of my reverie by a noise, a peculiar, truncated gurgle coming from Harpoonian. Something strange was happening to his face. It was contorted and twitching, his eyes squeezed shut, and then tears began seeping out of the eye cracks, and then it was a gusher, the tears rolling freely down his creased cheeks. I had seen him *almost* cry before, especially when he was talking about his mother, or his father who had died young. But I had never seen anything like this.

Struggling, he got himself under control. He took a big white handkerchief from his back pocket, blotted his eyes, then fanned them dry with the hanky. He blew his nose.

"These bastards are gonna ruin my company," he said between deep breaths. "The company I built with my own hands. They're gonna ruin it."

"It's their problem now," I said. My voice sounded like it was coming from a long way off, hollow and unfamiliar, from a dark cavern inside my brain.

"I made this place." He shoved the handkerchief back into his pocket. "My sweat. My effort. My life. And they're gonna fuck it up, sure as shit." He pushed violently against his desk, making his chair roll back and crash into the credenza behind him. "I never should have sold."

We were both quiet again. Then I said, "You've earned a rest."

His anger was spent.

"I don't need a rest." He put his head in his hands and stared down into the top of his desk. "I sold my life for thirty pieces of silver," he said, without looking up.

*   *   *

As I passed his office the next morning, Harpoonian motioned for me to come in.

"Here," he said, pushing a few bills into my hand. "Get me a bagel from the machine, okay? And a piece of fruit?"

He was wearing the same shirt he'd worn the day before, slightly rumpled now, and he'd taken off his tie. There was stubble on his chin. And did he actually smell a little stale?

"Marty, were you here all night?"

"And a coffee. Large, black. Hurry, okay?"

Harpoonian stayed in his office with the door closed and locked all day. I could hear his voice, muffled through the paneling, on the phone. I could tell who he was talking to by the tone of his voice, soft and soothing for Ethel, loud and raucous for one of his pals, loud and demanding for his lawyer, Meyer Kottman. Around three that afternoon he had a conversation loud enough for me to make out some of the words—*Fuck You*, and *Keep your fucking money*, and *It's off, it's off!*

A few minutes later my phone rang. It was Wolfe from 21st Century America again.

"Howard," he said, using my first name like we were old pals, "what's wrong with your ex-boss? He sounds a bit stressed."

"I can't speak for Mr. Harpoonian," I answered.

"No, but you can speak *to* him." When I didn't respond, he filled the silence, as if uncomfortable with letting it go on too long. "How many years have you been with Harpco, Howard?"

"A little over fifteen."

"We're going to need good people, Howard. Folks who know the business. Good people we can rely on."

"Yes," I replied.

"Are you married?"

"Divorced."

"Well, that happens. Kids?"

"No," I lied.

"How much are you making now?" he asked.

I told him, although he knew damned well how much I made, how much every executive in the company made. I'd prepared the report for him myself.

"As soon as we're settled in, let's have lunch," he said.

"Sounds good," I said.

"In the meantime, Howard, could you talk to Marty for us? You've got his ear. Do us a favor. Ask him to be out over the weekend. He doesn't own Harpco anymore. He has no standing. Tell him."

"Can you give him a little time? It's hard for him right now."

"Help us out, Howard. We'd be very grateful. You understand."

Yes, I understood.

That evening, when I knocked on his locked door, Harpoonian would not look up from his desk.

* * *

On Friday morning he was still in his office, slumped in his chair, his eyes closed. His beard had roughened and his hair was matted in long clumps, as if he had doused his head with water and tried to comb it with his fingers. I could not tell if he was asleep or awake. Crumpled snack food wrappers and a couple of soda cans had been added to the chaos of his desk.

Taped to my office door was an envelope, "Send this back! M.H." written across it in Harpoonian's unmistakable scrawl. Inside was the ten million dollar check, VOID written across its face in fat, black magic marker. I slipped the envelope into my desk drawer.

Later that morning I heard Ethel's voice coming from Harpoonian's office. She spoke too softly for me to understand her, but I clearly heard the occasional interjection from her husband, a sharp, loud "No!" After about an hour, she left his office, her eyes moist and red.

Later that afternoon, son Jack came into my office. He sat down across the desk and stared at me for a while, maybe deciding whether or not I was trustworthy. He still had the soft, overfed features he'd had as a teenager. The son had not inherited the father's hardness and discipline, but he would inherit the millions.

"Come talk to Dad with me," he said finally.

"I don't think he'll let us in," I said.

"I know you have a key."

"He trusted me with a key," I said.

"Let's use it."

Harpoonian slowly raised his head as we came into his office, his puffy eyelids lifting like a drowsy turtle's. He stood up and stretched, then tried to flatten out the wrinkles in his shirt. There were large damp patches under his arms and his pants had lost their sharp creases. The air in the room was old, used, softly putrid.

"Dad."

"I'm not leaving," Harpoonian said, his voice rubbed raw. He sat back heavily into his chair.

"Mom is worried about you. She wants you home."

"This is my company. I'm not leaving."

"You sold it, Marty. You got ninety million. You can retire now. Relax."

"Barnacle, whose side you on?"

"Your side, Marty."

"They tricked me. I gave back the money." He snapped me a quick, hard look. "You take care of that check, Barnacle?"

Jack spoke before I had to answer. "They don't want the money back, Dad. They want the company. It's legally theirs."

"Jack, are you that dense? They'll just tear this company down and sell off the pieces."

The son absorbed the father's insult, and hurled one of his own.

"Dad, you're too ... fucking ... old," Jack said with a vehemence that surprised all three of us, and in the shocked silence that followed, I saw the slightest glimmer of the father in the son. Jack was taking deep breaths, and Harpoonian seemed to have stopped breathing altogether. Then he pretended to look for something on

31

his desk, shoving papers this way and that. Finally, he gave up the pretense, sat back in his big chair.

"I never should have sold. I'm not leaving."

"They're good managers," Jack said. "They have a track record."

"In six months you'll be gone, you schmuck. They'll throw your lazy ass out."

Jack went suddenly crimson.

"Dad, that's not necessary."

"Barnacle, too. And how about McCarthy and Dingler and Zatkoff? They've been with me for over thirty-five years." He was banging on the top of his desk with the tip of his stiffened index finger. "And two thousand people in the plants. My people. Hard workers. I sold them out."

Harpoonian went to one of the file cabinets and came back with a folder jammed with black and white photos. He began shuffling through them.

"Here, look." He tossed a picture across the desk at me. "The inside of my first shop. See those racks? I built 'em with my own hands. Me and McCarthy. Here, look." He pitched a photo towards Jack. "I was working eighteen, twenty hours a day then. For years." He tossed another picture towards me. "We were setting up equipment. Look, the Illinois plant. Can you believe it? Here, look." He tossed another picture. "The St. Louis plant, just a hole in the ground. Look, look, look," he said, tossing a series of photos at his son in quick succession. "My company. My life. My—my people." I thought he might cry again. "It isn't worth any amount of money."

Later that afternoon, Wolfe called.

"We hope he'll come to his senses and move out over the weekend."

"I hope so, too," I said.

*   *   *

On Monday, Harpoonian was still there. When I walked past his office he was standing at the file cabinets, his back towards the door as if he didn't want anyone to see him. More food wrappers were strewn across the desk, and a clutter of pop cans and empty coffee cups. His silk plaid sport coat was balled up at one end of the sofa, a pillow for his head while he'd slept on the thin pad. People walking past his office averted their eyes.

Taped to my office door was an envelope. Inside was a one hundred-dollar bill and a note. "Get me some shaving stuff, soap, toothbrush, etc—hairbrush, etc—towels. A couple of white shirts. 15½ - 33. Leave the bag in your office tonight. M.H."

"Howard, what are we going to do about my dad?"

Jack was standing in my doorway.

"Why should we do anything about him, Jack?" I said as I put the note back in the envelope.

"Howard, he's screwing everything up. Wolfe is losing patience."

"He's not our responsibility, Jack. What he does, he does."

"Howard, he's having a nervous breakdown for Chrissake! Can't you see that?"

"I don't think so."

"He's done a lot for you, Howard," he said with some anger, but his anger was pathetically weak compared to the rages his father could muster.

"He's a big boy. He's responsible for his own actions."

"Howard, he hasn't been home in five nights. He hasn't left his office, as far as I can tell, except to go to the john in the middle of the night."

"It seems that way."

"He's just eating junk. I don't know if he's taking his medicine. He takes medicine, you know."

"I know."

"For his prostate."

"I know."

"At least he's supposed to."

Later that morning Wolfe called.

"The transition is going smoothly," he said. "Don't you agree?"

New people had begun showing up in all of the departments, in accounting, in sales, in transportation, out in the plants and the warehouses. Everywhere except here, in the executive area. They couldn't move in here until Harpoonian moved out.

"Do you have any ideas how we might resolve this situation?" Wolfe asked.

"No."

"Help us out here, Howard. You know him well."

"You could ask Meyer Kottman to talk to him."

"They're old friends, right?"

"And maybe Mrs. Harpoonian could contact the priest from his church."

"Mrs. Harpoonian is a lovely woman," Wolfe said. "Are they Catholic?"

"St. George's Armenian Apostolic. Mr. Harpoonian is friends with Father Aram. Maybe he could talk to him."

"Excellent. Thanks. We appreciate your help, Howard."

"He gave me the ten million dollar check. He wrote *void* across it."

"No problem. Give it to Kottman when you see him."

"No problem."

"We'll issue another check."

That night, when I left the bag for Harpoonian, I wrote my own note and put it inside: "Don't forget your prostate medicine."

* * *

On Tuesday, Harpoonian was at his desk, clean-shaven, wearing a clean shirt. He was working on some papers, and seemed alert, his movements brisk and strong.

Sylvia, his secretary, came into my office.

"Somebody cut off the boss's phone," she said. "At the master controller, I guess."

During the next few days Harpoonian unlocked his door for Meyer Kottman, for several of his old business cronies, for old employees like McCarthy and Zatkoff, for his priest, for Ethel. On Thursday morning his grandchildren, Jack's kids, came by, a four-year-old and a seven-year-old. Harpoonian tickled them and bounced them on his knee and gave them candy and when they said, "Poppi, come home. We miss you." He laughed and tickled them some more and gave them more candy. Later, a Federal Marshall delivered some papers. Harpoonian tore the papers to pieces and threw them into the wastebasket. That afternoon the power to his office was cut off. No more lights. No TV.

*   *   *

On Friday he was wearing another clean shirt. He had found some empty boxes, had cleaned off his desk. It looked as if he was starting new, fresh.

Wolfe called again.

That evening, although I was the last person to leave the building, I did not turn on the security alarm. At one a.m. I returned, pulling my car up as close to the front door as possible. There were three other vehicles waiting, two dark sedans and a small van, and five men, young and efficient, all wearing dark pants, dark wind breakers and black sneakers. Two of them carried heavy black flashlights, not turned on. One carried a bag, like a doctor's bag. Wolfe was not among them.

There were no greetings. One of the men put a key up to the lock of the front door and looked at me. I nodded. He pushed the key in and turned it. We walked cautiously through the dark lobby and then single file up the stairs. The hallway was lit only by the red glow of an exit sign high on the wall at the landing. We paused a few steps from Harpoonian's door. One of the men held a penlight towards the floor, casting a weak circle of light. I took a key from my pocket and held it toward him. He shook his head *no* and pointed at me. I could not see his face.

I moved to Harpoonian's door, carefully slid the key into the lock and turned it. Then I went back to the stairs and waited.

There was a sudden burst of light as the two men turned on their flashlights and rushed through the office door. They were followed by the man with the doctor's bag. I heard Harpoonian call out, "What?" There was the sound of a short scuffle, then silence. The men who had been waiting in the hallway went inside. I read my watch by the glow from the exit sign at least a dozen times during the next few minutes.

Finally, two men came out, propping up Harpoonian between them. His head lolled sideways, there was a bit of drool seeping out of the corner of his mouth, and his eyes were barely open. His shirt was mis-buttoned, and hung out over his pants. His sleeve was pushed up, the gold Ebel hung limply at his wrist, and there was a Band-Aid on the inside of his arm. They had put his shoes on over his pale bare feet.

He looked towards me and mumbled my name, Barnacle, but I do not believe there were any deep thoughts going through his mind at that time. He merely recognized a familiar face and said my name. If he'd known what I'd done, he might have asked "why?" So I asked the question for him. And this was the best answer I could come up with—sometimes we just get caught up in the flow of things, not giving our actions, or their consequences, a lot of thought. We intend no malice, no betrayal of the ones we love. We simply move forward, taking what seems like the most appropriate path. Is it these seemingly inevitable acts we eventually regret the most?

They moved down the hallway, first the man with the doctor's bag, then the two men with flashlights, then Harpoonian slumped between the two others, the toes of his shiny black tassel loafers making parallel tracks in the carpet pile, and then they went down the stairs, the thump, thump, thump as his toes bounced from step to step.

*   *   *

I saw Martin Harpoonian only one more time, about a year later. It was on the day the wrecking company demolished the office and the main plant of Harpco Molds and Plastics. The buildings had been vacant for six months. I had come by to watch the destruction. I was standing on the sidewalk when I saw Harpoonian's big sedan moving slowly along the street. Ethel was driving. Harpoonian was in the passenger seat, shrunken it seemed, staring without expression out of the side window, staring out at the dust rising over the rubble.

About the Author

George Dila's short story collection, *Nothing More to Tell*, was published by Mayapple Press in 2011. His short stories and personal essays have appeared in numerous journals and earned several literary awards and prizes. A native Detroiter, he now lives and writes from the Lake Michigan shore town of Ludington.

Also from
One Wet Shoe Publishing

Kayfabe & Other Stories by Saul Lemerond, 2013
Paper, 110 pp., $15.95, plus s&h.
ISBN 978-0-989607-10-0
eBook, $7.95

Cuttyhunk: Life on the Rock by Margo Solod, 2011
Paper, 298 pp., $19.95, plus s&h.
ISBN 978-0-615485-39-3
eBook, $9.99

For a complete listing of One Wet Shoe Media publications,
please visit our website at
www.onewetshoe.com. Books and eBooks can be ordered direct
from our website with secure
on-line payment using PayPal, or by mail
(check or money order).